My Afro
Twin Best Friends

written by
Tiana-Rose Akoh-Arrey

illustrated by
Bryony Dick

First Printed in United Kingdom 2021

Published by Conscious Dreams Publishing
www.consciousdreamspublishing.com

Edited by Elise Abram

Illustrated by Bryony Dick

Designed/Typeset by Bryony Dick
ISBN: 978-1-913674-74-8

Dedication

Dedicated with love to children struggling
with loving something about their looks.
You are unique and beautiful - remember that.

'It's hair day again!' says Mummy.

'Oh, no. My 'fro! Mummy, can we just wash it and put in pigtails like Aaoki?' asked Tia. 'She is my best friend and I want to wear similar clothes and have similar hair styles. We want to be fashionable, but our hair is not the same. Help!'

'But we must comb through and moisturise,' Mummy replied.

Tia got a fright every time she saw her mum carry the hair bag downstairs.

Mummy gently teased Tia's hair, took out the plaits, and gently massaged every single bundle of hair.
'Ouch! Ouch! Ouch! Mummy. It hurts!' she screamed.

'Look how big your 'fro has become. It's beautiful,' said Mummy, handing her a looking-glass.

'Goodness gracious—my hair is bigger than last time!' Tia stared at her reflection in the mirror and spun around to her mummy.

'But can I have it in pigtails instead, Mummy? Aaoki has pigtails, and we like our hair similar. That's why we are twin best friends.'

Tia was never ready for hair-time. Hair time was very scary. Her afro-nappy hair was massive, and she couldn't get the comb through all by herself, so Mummy was always the hair fixer.

To get ready for school, Mummy quickly put Tia's hair up in a messy bun, and off to school she went.

In morning assembly, Mrs Smith announced that there was an infestation of lice in Tia's year group. The children would have to keep their hair neat and tidy, have their hair locked in neat plaits or cut their hair to prevent lice.

Tia couldn't believe it. Her mind raced. 'Oh, my 'fro! Oh, my 'fro!' Tia's mind screamed.

Great Fire of Lo

YEAR 2

PUDDING LANE

Her friend Aaoki came over to her seat, smiling. Her hair was drawn neatly up into beautiful pigtails. Her braids shimmered softly in the dim classroom lighting.

"Hi, Tia. You look sad. What's the matter?"

"What if I have lice? I wish my hair was as soft as your hair. I'm afraid that my messy hair will catch lice, and we won't have our matching looks for picture day."

Aaoki made a face and said, "It hurts because you don't let your mum braid it. I let my mum braid mine. It hurt when she started, but gradually stopped hurting, and made my hair grow fast."

"But you have Indian hair," Tia responded, almost sobbing. "Your hair is so soft, and it doesn't tangle."

"You must try, Tia. What if you catch lice and your mum needs to give you a haircut?"

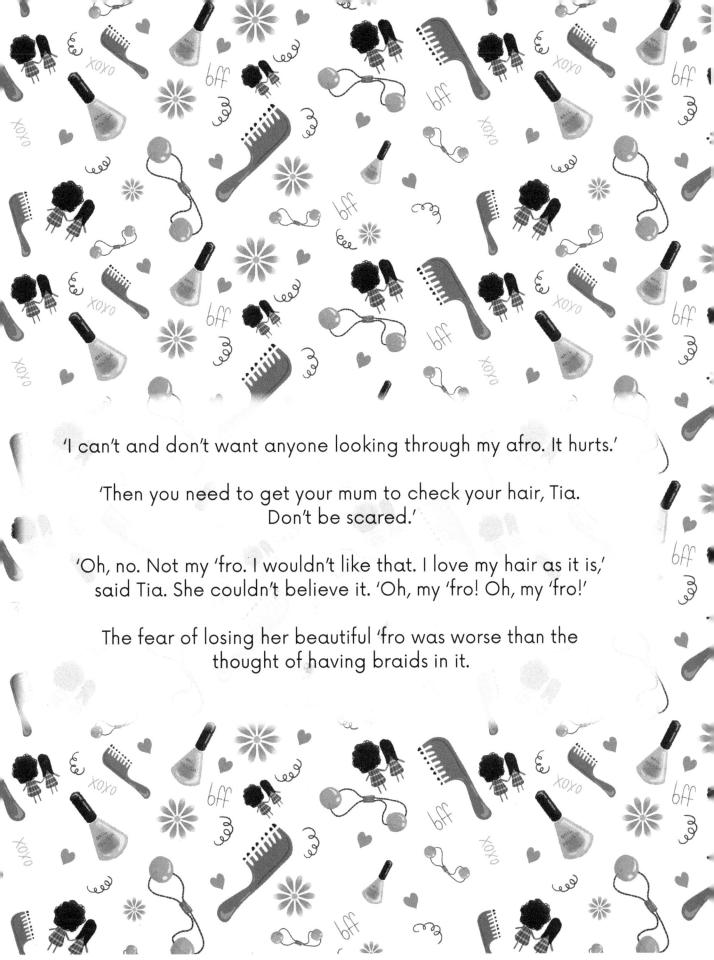

'I can't and don't want anyone looking through my afro. It hurts.'

'Then you need to get your mum to check your hair, Tia. Don't be scared.'

'Oh, no. Not my 'fro. I wouldn't like that. I love my hair as it is,' said Tia. She couldn't believe it. 'Oh, my 'fro! Oh, my 'fro!'

The fear of losing her beautiful 'fro was worse than the thought of having braids in it.

There were so many options for her hair.

She could wear it in plaits.
She could have cornrows.
She could have her 'fro in a ponytail or pigtails.
She could also have it as a gorgeous afro.

Her hair was magical and could take many forms. Her mummy
had always reassured her, with a little bit of water and
moisturiser her hair could take many different styles.

'Okay. I'll get my mummy to braid it today, then,' Tia told Aaoki, smiling.

When Mum picked her up from school, Tia asked, 'Mummy, can you braid my hair, please? I promise I will be brave.'

'Are you sure, Tia?'

'Yes. If you don't, I might catch lice, and you'll have to chop off my beautiful 'fro.'

'That's my girl,' Mummy said.
She scooped Tia into her arms, and they spun and laughed together.

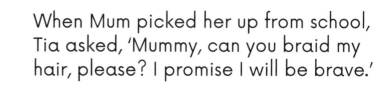

'What style would you like me to do on your hair?'

'Look, Mummy—Aaoki's style: two plaits all the way down my shoulder so we can complete our twin best friend look.'

On picture day, Tia and Aaoki sat on the swings,
staring at each other excitedly, wearing:

similar shoes,
the same uniform,
the same school jumpers,
and the same hairstyle.

They were truly like twins.

After picture day, Tia wore her hair back in a neat 'fro. She was happy to be able to do the twin look for picture day with Aaoki <u>and</u> return to her beautiful Afro hair.

Her hair was truly magical and made her feel super special.

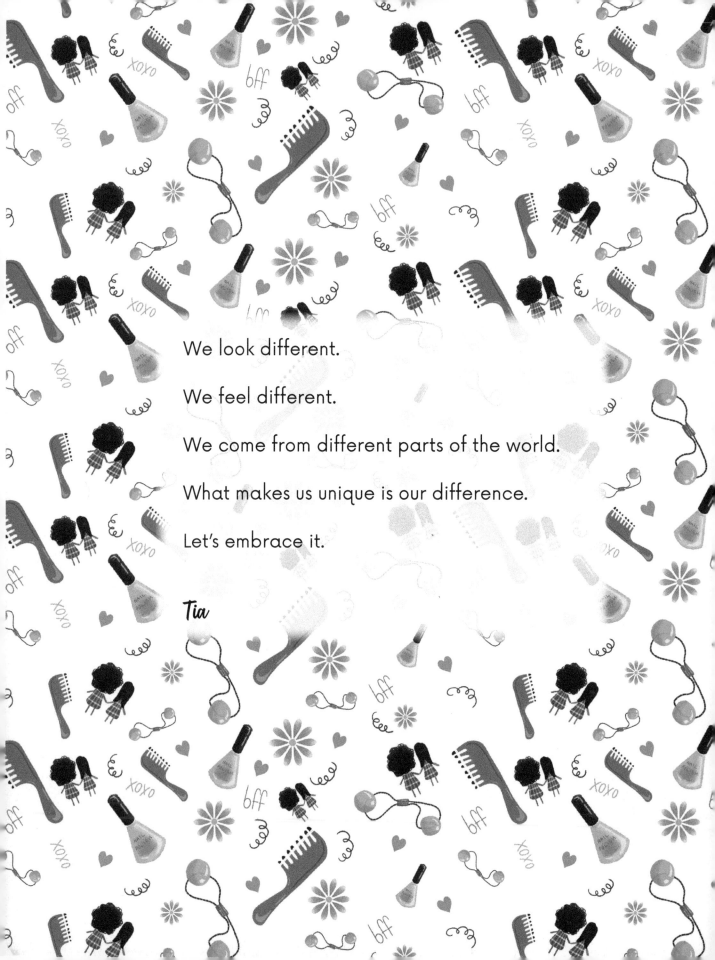

We look different.

We feel different.

We come from different parts of the world.

What makes us unique is our difference.

Let's embrace it.

Tia

About the Author

Hello, my name is Tiana-Rose and this is my first book. I am seven years old. I love writing, drawing and dancing. At the age of five, I started having writing classes with my mum who edited and guided me through writing short stories. I'd love to publish many more books. Although I love science and think I'll be a scientist, being an author is my first passion.

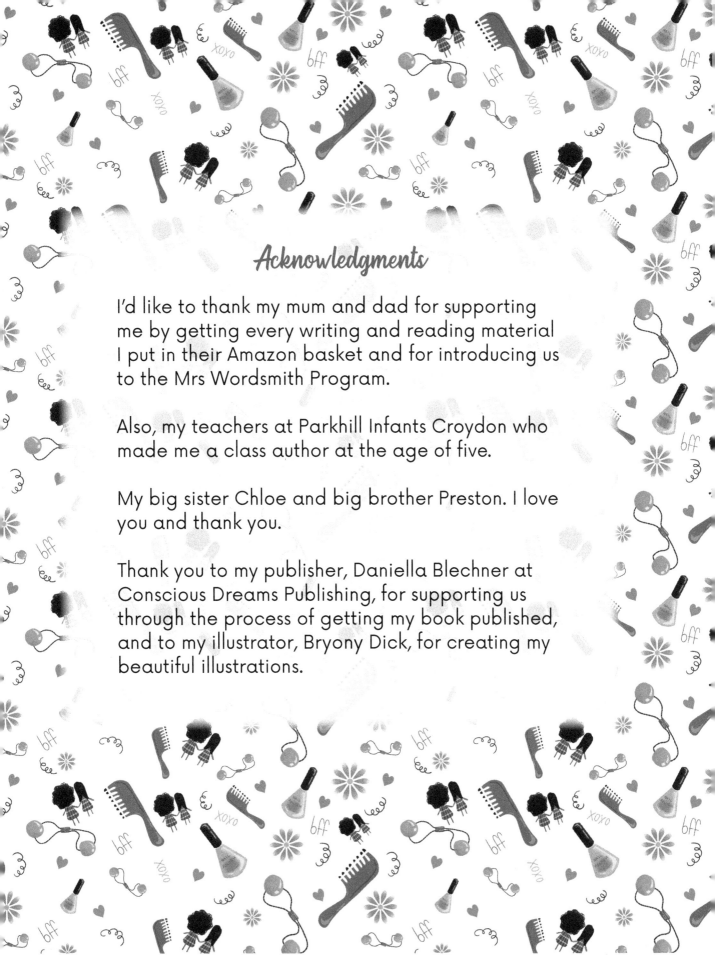

Acknowledgments

I'd like to thank my mum and dad for supporting me by getting every writing and reading material I put in their Amazon basket and for introducing us to the Mrs Wordsmith Program.

Also, my teachers at Parkhill Infants Croydon who made me a class author at the age of five.

My big sister Chloe and big brother Preston. I love you and thank you.

Thank you to my publisher, Daniella Blechner at Conscious Dreams Publishing, for supporting us through the process of getting my book published, and to my illustrator, Bryony Dick, for creating my beautiful illustrations.

Conscious Dreams
PUBLISHING

Be the author of your own destiny

www.consciousdreamspublishing.com

info@consciousdreamspublishing.com

Let's connect

Lightning Source UK Ltd.
Milton Keynes UK
UKHW050126301221
396342UK00003B/87